UNEARTHED

Richard Chizmar

Ray Garton

Brian Keene

Published by Apokrupha

All stories copyright, 2016
ISBN: 978-1534941090

Cover Design by Elderlemon Design
elderlemondesign.com

apokrupha.com

Table of Contents

The Good Old Days   1

The Sculptor
   with Ray Garton   6

Roses and Raindrops
   with Brian Keene   35

Writer Biographies

UNEARTHED

The Good Old Days

Richard Chizmar

Back in the late 1980's—yeah, I know, many of you weren't even alive back then—the horror scene was a happening place. New York publishing was booming and there were horror-specific imprints from TOR and NAL and Zebra and Leisure. Each month brought a wide variety of new horror titles, and themed and unthemed mass-market anthologies overflowed bookstore shelves. You could even still find pro magazines like *The Twilight Zone* and *Omni* at your local newsstand.

But, for me, the small press was where the most vital work was being published in the horror genre. You had a proliferation of quality specialty book publishers (Dark Harvest, Ziesing Books, Underwood-Miller, Donald Grant) and semi-pro mags that were every bit as entertaining—and difficult to sell to—as the big boys. I'm talking about *The Horror Show, Midnight Graffiti, New Blood, Grue, Deathrealm*, and several others. And then there were the really small—but no less enjoyable and devoted—publications like my own *Cemetery Dance* and *Thin Ice* and *Portents* and *Doppelganger* and *Eldritch Tales* and many many more.

If you're starting to get the picture that the late 80's was a great time to be a horror fan and writer, you're right on target.

I was there. I lived—and loved—every minute of it.

I sold my first short story in 1987. I was a twenty-year-old college student at the time. The story was a the-devil-comes-to-small town, Stephen King imitation, and, after only a handful of rejections, it sold to a California-based publication called *Scifant*.

I remember that was a very good day.

Over the next several years, I racked up dozens and dozens of rejections (from pretty much every pro and semi-pro magazine I mentioned above) and many more sales (to most of the smaller publications I mentioned above and a stack of others, including the ever-gracefully-titled *Festering Brain Sores* magazine).

In addition to *The Horror Show*, the magazine I most wanted to land a story with back in those days was Chris Lacher's *New Blood*. The magazine looked spectacular and Lacher paid professional rates and had published good stories by many of my favorite authors at the time; guys like Ray Garton (his first short fiction sale, I believe) and Bill Relling and Dave Silva. They were graphic tales that didn't flinch from violence or sexuality or even downright deviance. It certainly wasn't my usual fiction flavor, but I was young and energetic and determined to crack the *New Blood* vault—something I finally did, after something like ten rejections, in 1990 with a nasty little tale called "Roses and Raindrops."

I remember several things about that special sale:

1. Chris Lacher offered some wonderful suggestions that made the story better (I still have the marked-up manuscript in my files);
2. It was my biggest sale to date, and Kara and I celebrated with a steak and shrimp dinner;
3. I was devastated a short time later when *New Blood* closed down before the story could appear within its pages.

For reasons unknown to me then and now, I never submitted "Roses and Raindrops" to anyone else after it was returned to me. For over two decades, it sat in my files. Forgotten.

Until a couple months ago, when I stumbled upon the old, yellowed manuscript—and several others—tucked away in a dusty file at my home office.

Finding and rereading those old stories—written at a time when Cemetery Dance Publications and my marriage and the birth of my boys and so many other life-altering moments—weren't even a flicker in my mind truly felt like taking a ride back in a time machine.

So many amazing memories came rushing over me, and I sat there and let them, remembering my old Apple computer; my dot-matrix printer; my beat-up desk and the first-floor apartment window I used to stare out of when my imagination was really working; the Post Office box I would rush to every afternoon to retrieve my mail; all the rejections; and the acceptances.

It really was a wonderful time to be young and full of dreams.

The first manuscript I pulled out and read that day was "Roses and Raindrops." It was rough around the edges (boy, was it) and very much in the vein of an EC Comics tale (as were most of my early story sales), but it was also something else—it was clearly a product of those heady horror days of the late 80's, and more importantly, it was *fun*. When I finished reading it, I decided I still liked the story quite a bit and immediately considered rewriting it.

I even sat down one afternoon and started. But then I had a change of heart—and a much better idea. I thought: *why don't I send the story to one of the other writers who grew up during that time period and ask them to rewrite it? Someone who was doing the exact same thing I was doing back in the late 80's—churning out stories and stuffing them in envelopes with return postage and sending them off on their way with a hope and a prayer.*

The first person I thought of in regards to "Roses and Raindrops" was Brian Keene. Talk about a guy who has worked in the trenches and paid his dues. I wasn't sure if Brian would be receptive (he's a pretty busy dude; ahem), so I was thrilled when he immediately and eagerly agreed to collaborate on the story. He even told me that he'd also been a big fan and had tried to crack *New Blood* magazine for many years himself. Once I'd heard that, I knew I'd made the right choice.

The second manuscript I took out of the file and read was a lengthier tale called "The Sculptor." Right away, I remembered that it was my college roommate's favorite story of mine back then, and that it had never sold (so much for my buddy's good taste). To my surprise and delight, I found myself still liking the story. Much like "Roses and Raindrops" it was a simple, fun, throwback horror tale.

And I had the perfect writer in mind to rewrite it: Ray Garton.

Remember when I mentioned above that Ray had sold his first-ever short story to *New Blood*? Even at such a young age, Ray was a big deal back then. Still barely twenty years old, his debut novel, *Seductions*, had already been published in mass-market and Garton classics such as *Live Girls* and *Crucifix Autumn* weren't far behind. Ray was a master at writing about every day folks down on their luck and faced with otherworldly obstacles. I knew he would be perfect for "The Sculptor."

Ray Garton and Brian Keene. I'm immensely grateful to both these guys…not only for years of entertainment and support and friendship, but for answering my calls and agreeing to come out and play with me (and my two stories from a long-ago time).

Both Ray and Brian are better writers than I am, and the stories show it.

The three of us had a blast, and we hope you do, too.

-Richard Chizmar
July 2016

The Sculptor

Richard Chizmar & Ray Garton

"How's it going, Alex?"

"Don't ask, Marcus, you don't want to know. Give me the usual."

"Still can't work?" Marcus said as he scooped ice into a glass and poured the bourbon.

Alex shook his head. "Nine months."

He lifted the glass to his lips, intending to sip. Instead, he finished it off in a couple of swallows and placed the glass back on the bar. "Keep 'em coming."

It was a dark little hotel bar called the Black Diamond in Alex's neighborhood, with shiny mahogany and backlit hanging plants. Not especially stylish, but comfortable and quiet. He loathed the sound of people having fun when he was miserable. Twinkling piano music came from the corner, where a lovely Asian woman was seated at the old piano.

"She's new," Alex said. "It's nice. I like it."

Marcus smiled. "She plays a lot of the old stuff I love, she's good, and I told her she's welcome here anytime." He leaned his hands on the bar, arms spread, a rotund black man with a bald crown and a lot of salt in his pepper fringe. "Sorry about the work, man. Must be tough to run out of ideas."

"No, it's not that." He knocked back another drink and Marcus poured. "The ideas are still there, the urge is—no, the *need* to sculpt is still there. But I've...I don't know, somehow I've lost my connection to it, or something. But it's still in there, squirming and clawing. Trying to get out." He lifted the glass. "That's why this has become such a good friend." He took a sip.

Marcus's eyes darkened with worry. "You sure you're okay? You know, I don't close tonight. You slow down on that drinking, we can go out when I get off, have a few together."

He shook his head, then finished the drink. "I wouldn't do that to you, Marcus. I'm not good company for anybody tonight. I'm better off alone."

"Well, if you change your mind, you've got my number."

Alex tapped a finger on the edge of the glass. "Pour me another."

He jerked awake and sat up clumsily in bed, in the dark, with the feeling that thick tentacles were wrapped around his legs. He was merely tangled in the covers and a little sweaty, even though it was a chilly night. He had been awakened by a noise.

It was a scratching sound, but it stopped the moment he sat up, if it had been there at all. He listened to the night's silence, wondering if he had dreamed it. It probably was Sophie, his Siamese cat. She often had bursts of energy at night and ran through the place as if pursued. He lay back and rested his head on the pillow. He had been quite drunk when he'd gone to bed earlier that night, so drunk he couldn't remember going to bed at all, and his head was still thick, his stomach still queasy.

The sound came again, louder this time, a harsh scraping sound, as if something heavy were being moved in increments over the floor. Something much heavier than Sophie. It came from the direction of his studio down the hall.

Alex rose up again, extracted his legs from the clutching covers, and sat on the edge of the bed. Although he normally slept in the nude, he found he was still wearing his boxers.

He lived in an ancient, remodeled warehouse that consisted of four separate rooms and an enormous open studio space. It was cold and drafty that night, so he stood, took his robe from a chair beside the nightstand, and slipped it on as he stepped into a pair of old flip-flops. He swayed for a moment and almost sat on the bed again because he was still drunk and not too steady on his feet. Instead, he headed for the door and stopped when he heard the sound again.

Fully awake now, the fact that someone else was in the house cut through his alcoholic haze like a razor and made him feel an inner chill unrelated to the room's temperature. He turned back to the nightstand, opened the top drawer, and removed the loaded .38 pistol he kept there.

He opened the bedroom door, leaned out, and looked in both directions. The hall was empty. The soft light he always left on over the stove fell through the open kitchen doorway. He saw no one, no sign of anyone. Stepping out of the doorway, he turned left and started toward the closed studio door at the end of the hall, his flip-flops slapping softly against his heels as he walked. Drunkenness gone now, vaporized by a sudden surge of fear, Alex felt hyper-alert. A bead of sweat trickled down his temple and his heartbeat increased as the door of the studio grew larger in his view.

The terrible scraping noise came again and Alex froze, fist clenched on the butt of the gun.

Losing my reason for living wasn't enough, he thought. *I needed a home invasion to top it all off. Maybe he's armed and he'll end it for me, get the whole damned thing over with.*

He started forward again.

Two weeks after his thirty-second birthday, Alexander Lynn Cason made the jump from the ripped blue jeans, long-haired, unemployed freak world of sidewalk sculptors to the highly respected and deliriously lucrative world of the *artiste*. His award-winning black-granite statue of two Vietnam infantry grunts lifting a wounded comrade to the outstretched arms of a Huey helicopter medic had allowed his foot to slip firmly in between the success threshold and the constantly slamming door of rejection.

More significant work followed, and before he had time to catch his breath, he was being featured in dozens of art publications and was even covered by pieces in *Time* and *Newsweek*.

Four years later, in a festive, televised ceremony in the nation's capital, Alex celebrated the pinnacle of his new career when, during the traditional Fourth of July ceremony, his eighteen-foot statue of George Washington was unveiled in front of the Washington Monument, and Alex captured the heart of a patriotic America.

The big-ticket commissions continued to pour in and he was able to choose his work more selectively. Over the next four years, he worked just twice—a bust for a Harvard Law School library and an eccentric billionaire's life-size sculpture of George Armstrong Custer making his last stand at the Little Big Horn, both of which earned him enough money to focus on personal projects in his home studio for a while. These creations were not for sale and were rarely even shown to the public. They simply kept his skills, vision, and soul happy and content.

Until nine months ago, when the troubles began.

Initially, he began having problems concentrating on his work. His usually sharp and clear vision felt blurred and sluggish. Then, slowly, his ability to sculpt left him a piece at a time. It was like parts of his body falling off. He was quickly, systematically stripped of the skills that allowed him to create and the inspiration that brought those skills to life. He was suddenly a novice once again, all of his experience vanished as if it had never been, replaced by feelings of self-doubt and a sense of crippling inadequacy.

At first, he thought a part of him had died, but that was not accurate. As he had explained to Marcus, his favorite bartender, the thing inside of him that was released when he created something special was still there, still alive and squirming. But it was trapped. Somewhere deep inside him, it was bound and writhing and suffocating, in a tight cocoon.

Alex told no one. He had no family and no close friends, only acquaintances. Marcus was the closest thing he had to a real friend. Alex had learned at an early age not to trust easily—from his parents. They were textbook alcoholics, never physically abusive, but always neglectful. The three words he remembered most clearly from his childhood were not "I love you." Instead, they were a cold and dismissive: "Not my problem."

So, he had told no one of his troubles. He had even kept it from his agent and his manager and let all calls go to voicemail. After a while, he stopped checking his messages and email, and he never answered his door. He was completely alone with his suffering.

The previous evening, he had tried one final time to find his muse and create something. *Anything*. For two hours, he'd worked with a block of clay, searching for the *thing* hidden inside, waiting for the spark of inspiration that would find it. The inspiration did not come and the block of clay yielded nothing.

And yet, inside of Alex, it still squirmed.

Frustrated, he had gone for a walk through the park, along the canal, then hit some bars on the way home, an activity he had been engaging in with increasing frequency over the past six weeks. His last memory before being awakened in bed was of one of those bars. He could not even remember which one it was. Only that he had vomited in a toilet stall in a filthy bathroom.

He wanted—*needed*—to sedate that thing inside him, make it

stop writhing, but before he could accomplish that, he had sedated himself into a blackout. It had not been the first time and he feared it would not be the last. His work had been his life, but that life seemed to be over now. Drinking helped to numb the pain of his loss. Drinking helped him forget.

Alex turned the knob, pushed the door open, and looked into the silent, mineshaft-black darkness of his studio. The gun felt heavy in his right hand as he aimed it into the darkness. He reached his left hand over it, found the two light switches just inside, and flipped them up.

The sudden brightness blinded him, and he shielded his eyes with his forearm. After taking a moment to adjust, he lowered his arm and saw it. The gun forgotten at the end of his suddenly limp arm, he whispered, "What the hell?"

Centered in the middle of his studio was an enormous block of rough, uncut granite of exquisite quality. He estimated it was ten feet tall, eight feet wide.

He lowered his eyes to the rough grooves in the wood floor forming a path that extended three feet from the granite, then stopped. It was as if the slab had been lowered onto the floor from above, or had somehow risen up through the floor from below, then had been pushed or dragged for three feet to the center of the studio.

That was the sound he had heard. But how had the slab been moved? And by whom? It would have to have been a *team* of people with the appropriate equipment. He looked around the room slowly. There were no hiding places in his studio; it was a vast, open space, quite well-lit, and there was no one in it.

Something brushed softly against his bare calves and he reflexively leaped forward into the studio with a startled yelp. He spun around to see Sophie sitting in the doorway cleaning her face after a midnight snack. She stood and stared at him from the doorway for a moment, then turned and padded back down the hall, her tail a bouncing question mark.

Alex turned to the enormous block of granite—he was closer to it, now—as frantic warnings tumbled through his head. *Get out of here, leave, just turn around and go, because something's wrong here, something's very wrong.* Closing his eyes tightly, he thought, *I'm still drunk. That's all. This isn't happening.*

When he opened his eyes, the stone was still there. He walked closer, reached out a trembling hand to touch it, then abruptly pulled it back. *Not yet,* he thought without knowing why.

Alex took a few more steps until he was only inches from the stone. Narrowing his eyes slightly, he closely examined the surface. It was perfect, the finest granite he had ever seen. He yearned to touch it. But still, he did not.

How did it get here? And why?

He stepped around the slab and walked to the row of windows along the wall beyond. He raised the blinds on one of them and looked out into the night, trying to understand the presence of the enormous block of granite. There was no one outside, the narrow street on which the window looked upon was deserted, with only the dim glow of a single streetlight cutting through the darkness.

Turning away from the window, he began to pace, eyes never leaving the block of stone. Minutes passed. An alien, unfamiliar sensation rose slowly within him. Sweat rose on his forehead and upper lip in tiny glistening gems. His body trembled as if he had come down with a fever, and his pacing slowed to a stop as he began to feel unsteady on his feet. He wondered vaguely if he was getting sick.

He wanted to touch the stone, feel it against his skin. He already could feel the rough edges against his palms in his mind. He wanted to hammer away at it, cut into it. The warning voice came again: *No, don't do it, get out of the studio, lock it, and have someone come haul it off!* But he was distracted by the sudden awareness of his own heart beating, of his blood rushing through his veins.

He hurried to one of his work tables, placed the gun on it, and flung open a wide drawer. Inside were his hammers and chisels. Quickly, before he could change his mind, he snatched up one of each and turned back to the granite.

It stood there, a great monolith of pale stone. Waiting for him.

He took a step forward, then stopped, and turned back to the work table. Among the tools and jars, he spotted a half-full pint of bourbon that he had left there recently. He put his tools down, picked up the bottle, unscrewed the cap, and took several long, sloppy gulps, nearly emptying it before plopping it back onto the table.

He wiped his lips with the back of his hand and approached the block of stone, putting both tools in his left hand. When he reached out this time, he did not pull back. Instead, he softly placed his right palm against the rock. Immediately, he felt a surge of warm energy rush from the stone into his hand and throughout the rest of his body, a tingling that traveled through his arms, down his torso, and into his genitals. As his penis swelled, his mind was hit by a raging storm of ideas and emotions that swirled and coalesced, then moved with an inaudible hum downward through his arms and into his hands, where it burned for release. Something else in him swelled, as well, something at his very center. The part of him that was truly Alex experienced something familiar, something that happened often when he was working and being creative: the growing awareness of something bigger than himself that was coming *from* himself.

His hand slowly caressed the granite, as if the rough, hard surface were the velvety skin of a forbidden lover. He closed his eyes and felt the stone through his entire body, with all of his nerves.

The room began to spin, slowly at first, then faster. When he opened his eyes, it was still spinning. Everything in the room—the row of windows, the overhead lights, the tables—melted together into a swirling, kaleidoscopic blur around him. Only his hand and the stone remained stationary before him.

Run! Now! Before it's too late!

He switched the hammer to his right hand, placed the tip of

the chisel against the granite, and did not move for a while. Then he brought the hammer down and a jagged chunk dropped to the floor with a thud. He struck again and another piece of stone fell away.

Soon, he was hammering at a feverish pace, only vaguely aware of his blurry surroundings as they spun around him, as if in a trance, locked away in some deep part of his mind with nothing more than a narrow tunnel of vision focused on the stone and chisel. As the tunnel gradually narrowed and everything darkened, it occurred to him that it was just like the old days, back when he worked tirelessly, creating intensely. But that was not true. It was not like the old days. It was better. It had never been so easy.

Alex woke on the floor in his underwear, shivering in the cold, gray, morning light shining through the one window with raised blinds. He lay amid chunks of powdery dust and chipped stone, head pounding, feeling like he had a knife buried to the hilt in his neck.

He groaned as he lifted himself groggily off the floor onto his hands and knees. He turned his head and squinted at the digital clock on one of the tables. It was 1:11 in the afternoon. That meant he had been lying on the studio floor for—he did not know when he fell asleep, only that it was dark. He could not remember falling asleep or what he was doing at the time. Or anything else, for that matter.

He groaned and muttered curses as he struggled to his feet, punished by his aching muscles for every movement. As he pushed himself to his feet, a sharp, stabbing in his right hand almost made him fall to the floor again. Once standing, he examined his hand and found that the end of his thumb was purple and swollen and had blood caked around the nail. In the meaty pad of his thumb there was a small, red pinprick.

Alex tried to remember injuring his thumb, but as before, he could remember nothing about what he was doing before going to sleep. Looking down at his thumb, he saw the rubble of sculpting all around his feet. Tossed beyond it was his robe in a pile on the floor.

Then he remembered.

He turned around and faced the granite, looked at what he had done, and staggered backward, muttering, "Jesus Christ." He stepped back further, gawking at his work with a slack jaw and wide eyes.

I couldn't have done this. Not this much detail. Not with just a hammer and chisel. Not in one night.

"Impossible," he whispered.

But there was no other explanation. He looked around on the floor and spotted the hammer and chisel lying among ash-colored dust and chunks of stone. He found his flip-flops nearby and slipped his feet into them, then turned to the granite again.

Although he had no memory of it, Alex somehow had carved the lower portion of the slab. Two thick, powerful legs had been chiseled out of the granite from just below the waist to the ankles. He had finished neither the body from the waist up nor the feet, nor the gap between the legs. Hanging on each side of the legs was the lower half of a muscular arm. But the limbs were not those of a human being.

The arms and legs were covered with tiny scales that appeared to come to sharp points. Each scale had been carefully chiseled out of the stone. The scales gave way to a smoother texture around the wrist and on the hands—if they could be called hands. They more closely resembled claws, with seven long, slender fingers from which curved deadly talons.

Alex spotted a crimson smear on one of the pale talons and leaned close to inspect it. *That's what I cut myself on last night*, he thought, looking down at his injured thumb.

He crouched to look at the legs. They were like tree trunks, with smaller scales than the arms. They stopped at the ankles and ended in the base of the block of granite.

Standing unsteadily, he rubbed the back of his aching neck and surveyed his work. While he was glad that the muse had returned to him last night, something about it did not sit right with him. He still did not know where the granite had come from.

As he turned, he spotted the pint of bourbon on the table. *That stuff really kicked my ass last night,* he thought as he headed for the shower.

After a shower, some coffee, a hard-boiled egg, and half of an English muffin, Alex returned to the studio feeling refreshed by the shower and invigorated by last night's accomplishment. He turned on some Prokofiev and settled into his work environment, looking forward to experiencing the same fervor that obviously had driven him last night.

But when he picked up his hammer and chisel, they felt foreign in his hands, useless objects with which he had no connection. He placed the chisel against the stone and poised his hammer to strike, but he felt nothing. The urge to strike with the hammer, penetrate the stone, and cut and shape it into something it was not before, was simply not there. It felt like trying to eat when he was not hungry. The need was absent, and it was not, he had found, something that he could summon on command. Not anymore.

His hands fell to his sides, loosely clutching the useless tools. Head slumped forward, he looked down at his work from the previous night and yearned to do more. But he knew it was not going to happen now.

He left the studio, put on his coat, and went walking. He strolled along the canal, through the park, bought a bag of bread chunks to feed the ducks. As he left the park, he looked across the street at the old hotel that housed the Black Diamond, his favorite little bar, where Marcus poured the drinks and now a woman made pleasant music on the piano. Passing the hotel as he proceeded down the street, he found himself in the crosswalk at the end of the block, then he walked back the other way on the opposite side of the street.

He decided he would try to work again that night. When it was dark. Maybe that would help. And maybe a few drinks would help, too. They certainly had not slowed him down last night. He still couldn't believe what he had accomplished in one night.

He passed the entrance to the Sherman Hotel and went directly through the door to the Black Diamond and headed for the bar.

"Alex," Marcus nodded as he approached. "The usual?"

"The usual." He perched himself on a stool, took a handful of beer nuts from the bowl on the bar. "No music?"

"She comes in around five. Everything okay?"

"Yeah. Why?"

Marcus poured. "You don't mind my saying, you look like hell."

"Oh, yeah. That."

"Hung over from last night?"

"Partly that, partly exhaustion. I was up until...well, all night long, I guess. Working."

"Hey, congrats, man, you're getting some work done."

"More than that. The work is...I don't know, I woke up in the studio and—"

"You slept in your studio?"

"Well, I don't know if I curled up on the floor or just passed out, but that's where I woke up. And when I saw what I'd done...how *much* I'd done...in just one night..."

"What was it?"

Frowning down at the glass of amber, he shrugged. "I...I'm not sure. It's not done yet." He took a swallow of his drink.

Marcus stared at him for a moment, then asked, "You sure you're okay?"

"Yeah, sure. Why'd you ask again?"

"Because you look kind of, I don't know...*lost*. Like some abandoned kid, or something, I don't know."

Alex nodded slowly. "Funny you should say that. That's exactly how I feel when I can't work."

He stopped at a few bars on the walk home, the same bars he had visited the previous night before returning to his studio and becoming an artist again. Maybe he could capture it, whatever *it* was, and make some progress on that...thing.

Throughout his walk, while talking to Marcus, and drinking in bars, his mind kept returning to what he had created, to those sharp scales and enormous, seven-fingered hands with their menacing talons. It had not been derived from any of the images that had been occupying his mind as possible projects. It did not look like anything that had emerged from his imagination. People who knew his work probably would guess that it was not his at all.

And yet, he had sculpted it.

Alex walked home slowly because a part of him did not want to see the unfinished sculpture again.

It's not too late! Don't go back! Go to a hotel, somewhere, anywhere. But don't go back home.

And yet, his hands were twitching to get back to work.

The blinds on the window at the far end of the row were still up and the rectangle in the studio wall framed a segment of the night. The studio was silent until Alex, who lay on his side with his body curled in a childlike posture around the base of the granite, awoke with a scream and scrambled to his feet. He stumbled around for a moment before he realized where he was. He went to the window and stared out at the darkness, thinking, at first, that it was still night. But a narrow strip of murky light began to glow in the eastern sky. Dawn was coming. He turned around and looked at his work, walked slowly toward it, and stopped a few feet in front of it, head tilted back. What he saw twisted something inside his gut.

The creature had been fully revealed and towered over Alex. His ladder leaned against one side of it. He had no memory of moving the ladder or climbing it, but obviously he had because there it was, and obviously he had been busy because there the creature was, not quite complete yet—for one thing, its feet remained trapped inside the uncarved base of the stone—but exposed.

Two thick horns, like the horns of a great ram, curled from the sides of its head, and a short, squat horn sprouted from each of its broad, muscular shoulders. The creature seemed to be pulling its shoulders back, elbows bent at its sides, enormous, claw-like hands open as if ready to reach out. Its head was tilted downward so that the eyes, which seemed to be smiling, looked directly at Alex. Its nose was flat and stubby, with exposed nostrils above its most terrifying feature—an impossibly wide, lipless mouth open just enough to reveal the many jagged, protuberant fangs inside, and curled enough to form a subtle, cold smirk.

It was the best work he had ever done, and might very well turn out to be the finest work of his lifetime. But he had no memory of doing it, only aching muscles in his arms, back, and legs. The thing chilled his blood.

Alex turned and headed for the door to get something to drink and perhaps wash his face to clear his head, when he heard a sound that made him stop and listen.

Grinding. The gritty sound of stones grinding together.

He turned and made a whimpering sound when he saw that the statue's head had turned toward him. It was still watching him. A whimpering sound worked its way out of him.

The creature cocked its head as it stared at him and the movement left shimmering trails, lingering images of the head that blurred together as it moved. It reminded Alex of the time he tried acid in college, but there was no comfort in that because he knew he was not on acid now, just as he knew that he had created that thing with his own hands.

The grinding sound continued as the creature moved its jaw back and forth, trying it out, experimenting, as the large, reptilian eyes blinked, as the scoop-like hands flexed their long fingers. Then it turned to him again and began moving its mouth as if speaking, the lipless rims touching briefly, the black tongue making quick movements of articulation.

Alex made a hoarse sound of protest because he did not want to see what he was seeing, and he *certainly* did not want the thing to speak.

He heard nothing. But he *felt* things. He had thoughts that were not his own and felt the need to get Sophie. It was, quite suddenly, the most important thing in the world to him, finding Sophie, holding her to him.

The statue was forgotten instantly as he turned and hurried out of the studio and down the hall, calling the cat's name and making kissing sounds with his lips. He ducked into the bathroom, but the cat was not there. Nor was she in the kitchen, where her food and water bowls were kept. He found her curled up on his bed asleep.

"There you are, Sophie," he said as he scooped her up in his arms and held her close. She lifted her head and blinked her sleepy eyes as he carried her back down the hall. He felt immensely relieved to have found her as he carried her into the studio, stroking her as he spoke quiet nonsense to her until she was plucked away from him so quickly that she did not have a chance to make a sound.

Alex cried out in shock and lifted his head to see the creature bite down on the Siamese cat. He felt warm blood spatter his face.

He turned away, sickened, and as he began to walk in a frantic, confused circle in the studio, he found he could not stop screaming.

The following day, Alex found himself walking briskly and with purpose along the canal, the diamond patterns in the chain-link fence along the waterway flying by him in a blur. It was a gray, chilly day and it felt like rain. There was someplace he needed to be. He had no idea where, only that it was important that he get there. As he walked, he took his phone from his pocket and checked the time. Eight minutes before three.

He suddenly cut to the right, leaving the sidewalk to cross Canal Street, then he started down Chester Street, which joined Canal at a T intersection. On the first block, he passed a convenience store, a small strip mall, and an apartment complex, and on the next he passed a few small homes with front lawns and driveways. The moment he saw the school up ahead, he knew that it was his destination.

The Chester Street School was a red brick building with a narrow strip of lawn along the sidewalk in front and an American flag on a pole at the entrance to the path that led to front steps. As he approached, he saw no children in front of the school and knew he would have to wait a few minutes, and with that knowledge came the startling shock of realization: *It had sent him to get a child.*

Yesterday, it had made him scour the neighborhood for cats and small dogs. The creature had enjoyed Sophie and wanted more of the same. But after a day of those treats, it wanted something better. Something bigger.

Ever since it had awakened, it had been telling Alex to finish it. The words were not spoken aloud. The creature's abominable mouth moved in that blurry, acid-trip way and the words formed inside Alex's head in his own voice.

"*Finish me, Alex. Finish me now.*"

There was plenty of detail work left to do, enough to keep him busy on the creature between feedings. Enough to keep it silent. But the feet remained unfinished, still locked in the solid, flat base of the granite block. When it told him to finish, Alex knew it was referring to its feet. It wanted to walk. To be free.

What have I done? Alex thought as he stood staring at the school across the street. *What have I created?*

There was a fenced-in playground beside the school, empty now, the monkey bars and jungle gym and sliding board standing like the skeletons of exotic creatures in the gray light.

He removed his phone again and checked the time. The school bell would ring in four minutes. A moment later, the double doors in front would open and swarms of children would spill down the steps and over the front path.

Alex stepped off the sidewalk to cross the street, thinking, *I can't do this, I can't, there's no way.* But he moved forward, unable to stop himself. No, *afraid* to stop himself. If he tried to walk away, would the creature know? Did it have some kind of connection with him even five blocks away? And, if so, what would it do if he tried to resist? He was afraid to find out.

On the sidewalk, he strolled along the fence in front of the school looking no different than any other pedestrian. But inside he felt increasingly sick now that he understood why he was there.

Was this now his life? Fetching food for that thing? Keeping busy with touch-ups to avoid giving it feet so it couldn't walk free? Acting on its every whim?

The muted pealing of a bell came from the school.

The dogs and cats had been bad enough. Especially Sophie. Poor Sophie. He missed her so much.

You're going insane.

Alex kept his eyes on the double doors at the school's entrance.

Stop it now while you still can. Before you're a gibbering maniac.

The doors opened and children poured out of the building, down the broad steps.

Before you become a killer.

The children hurried down the path toward the sidewalk.

Go! Now! Run!

With a cry of panic lodged in his throat, Alex turned and ran. He braced himself for an explosion of the creature's anger inside his head, but it didn't come. Maybe he was too far away. Maybe the connection didn't extend very far, maybe not even beyond the studio.

The Black Diamond was just a few blocks over. He wondered if Marcus would be there at such an early hour.

Alex ran faster as it began to rain.

He entered the Black Diamond, soaking wet, as Marcus wiped down the bar. When he looked up and saw Alex hurrying toward him, out of breath, water dripping from his hair and down his face, Marcus stopped wiping and said, "What the hell happened to you?"

Alex bumped into the bar and nearly knocked over one of the stools as he panted for breath.

"Calm down, take a seat," Marcus said.

He perched himself unsteadily on a stool with both arms

resting on the bar. Suddenly overcome with emotion, he struggled not to cry.

"You're not gonna believe me, Marcus," he said. "You'll think I'm crazy."

"Let me get you a drink."

He put a glass of bourbon in front of Alex, who picked it up with a trembling hand and gulped it down. He thumped the glass onto the bar and stared at it a moment, thinking. Marcus would never believe what he had to say. Alex needed to *show* it to him.

"You have to come with me," he said.

"What? Where?"

"You've got to come to my place. I'll show you. If I tell you, you're gonna think I've lost my mind."

"I just got here and started my shift," Marcus said. "I can't take off now."

"Look, you've got to, because...because..."

His shoulders began shaking with sobs before he could get it under control and he lowered his head.

"Jesus, Alex, what's going on?"

He took a deep, steadying breath and lifted his head, looked at Marcus. "You're the closest thing I've got to a real friend in this town. You've got to help me. And to do that, you've got to come to the studio and see what...what I've done."

Marcus nodded slowly. "Okay...yeah...look, I'll ask Jerry to come out of the office and work the bar for an hour and we'll take off. Okay?"

Alex nodded and wiped the tears from his face.

Alex did not speak on the way to his place because he knew how crazy everything would sound. Marcus had an umbrella, but Alex hardly noticed the rain as he walked, then jogged, then walked again, while Marcus struggled to keep up.

Once inside, he took Marcus to the kitchen, where Alex removed his dripping coat and hung it on the back of a chair. Marcus did the same, and they sat at the table to catch their breath from the walk.

"Earlier in the week, I heard a sound in the middle of the night," Alex said. "At first, I thought it was the cat. But it turned out to be a huge block of granite in my studio. It wasn't there when I'd gone to bed, but it was there in the middle of the night all of a sudden, out of nowhere."

"Someone brought a block of granite—"

"Not just a block. It's at least ten feet high. It's huge."

"Then it must weigh—but where did it come from?"

"I don't know."

"You're saying someone brought it into your studio and just left it there? For no reason? That's crazy."

"See what I mean? Well, I went to work on it. The thing I—the *piece* that I did, it's...it's in there now. That's what I want to show you."

"Okay. Then why are we sitting in the kitchen?"

Alex leaned toward him and whispered, "Because I'm afraid of it."

Marcus looked at him silently for a moment, his face tense with concern. Then he said, "If I go in there with you, will you promise me something?"

"What?"

"When we're done in there, if I think you need to get some help—I'm just saying, you know, if I think you need to see a doctor, something like that—you'll do it. Deal?"

Alex was surprised by the flush of embarrassment he felt in his face as he nodded. "Yeah, I know, like I said, you'd think I was crazy if I told you everything first." He stood. "Let me show you."

They went down the hall to the closed door of the studio. As he unlocked it, Alex said, "One thing, and it's very important." He turned to look over his shoulder at Marcus. "If I say run, you run. Understand? You just get the hell out of here as fast as you can. Do you hear me?"

Keeping his face neutral, Marcus nodded.

Once in the studio, Alex heard Marcus gasp when he saw it.

The enormous figure stood in the original position in which Alex had carved it, but now the front of the pale creature was drenched in a crimson apron of blood that cascaded down from the chin and over the front of the body, dribbling in streams down the neck and throat, covering the belly and thighs. The tremendous hands were splashed with it, as was the base in which the creature's feet were still trapped.

"Jesus Christ, Alex, what have you done?"

"I told you, I went to work on the granite and—"

"No, the blood, all this *blood*."

"Oh, yeah. That. That's from the animals."

Marcus turned to him. "Animals?"

"Cats, small dogs. That's what I was afraid to tell you. See, this thing—"

Marcus squinted at him as if Alex suddenly had gone out of focus. "You've been sacrificing animals to this—"

"No, no, *no*. I *fed* them to him. I mean, he made me. He sent me out to get them. He...I don't know how...he gets inside my head and makes me...he makes me do things."

No longer squinting, Marcus looked hard at Alex as he slowly took a step backward, then another. "You're serious about this, Alex?"

"Yes! I'm telling you, it had me hunting for children earlier today. It wanted me to bring it a *child*. But I went to you instead. I didn't know what else to do."

Taking another step back, Marcus said, "You have to get help, Alex. Okay? You need to see somebody right away. You promised me you would, right?"

"Marcus, you've got to believe me. This thing, it's, I don't know, it's a—"

"Listen to me, Alex. This thing?" He reached up and placed a hand on the creature's stone arm. "It's a statue. That's all. It can't—"

Marcus screamed a heartbeat after he was lifted off the floor, but by then, it was too late. The creature had wrapped its enormous paw around Marcus's neck and lifted him to its widening mouth. It bit into Marcus's throat and neck as if it were biting into an apple.

Alex whimpered as Marcus's legs kicked and jittered. He slapped his hands over his eyes, but still heard the jagged, gargling screams, so he stuffed his hands over his ears and clenched his eyes shut. His head filled with the sound of his own sobs.

Later, once the studio was silent except for the slow, gentle dripping of blood from the statue, Alex picked up his hammer and chisel. He did not want to think about what he was doing very much because he was afraid he would think himself out of doing it, and he *had* to do it.

He imagined living the rest of his life the way he had lived the last few days and knew that he would rather die. If he had the courage to end it himself, he would, but he did not believe himself capable of it. Looking at the bloody claws at the end of his sculpture's muscular, scaly arms, he suspected it would not be a problem for the creature.

The studio reeked of blood and human waste, and Alex used his foot to nudge aside the remaining pieces of his friend, Marcus. They left gory smears on the floor. He crouched before the statue and placed the tip of the chisel against the granite base.

"*You're finishing me.*" It was Alex's own voice inside his head, but they were the creature's words.

"Yes," he said out loud.

"*You're freeing me.*"

"Yes."

"*Are you afraid?*"

"No. Yes. I am. Of course I am. But I can't live like this."

The room began to spin in a blur all around him, but his eyes remained focused on the rock. The sounds of the hammer striking the chisel and the chisel cutting into the stone filled his head until they were so loud that they would have drowned out the creature if it had spoken. But it remained silent as Alex worked, waiting patiently for its freedom. His focus became so intense that everything rushed together in the center of his field of vision and he was swallowed by blackness.

He rose slowly from the blackness, then emerged like a corpse bobbing to the surface of a still lake. Before opening his eyes, he wondered if he was still alive.

He was, once again, lying face-down on the cold floor of his studio, muscles aching. It was colder than usual, bitingly cold. Pushing himself slowly to his knees, he wondered *why* he was still alive and suspected he had lost consciousness before finishing the job. He stood, swayed dizzily for a bit, then turned around.

The statue was gone.

He quickly looked all around the studio and his eyes fell on the great hole in the wall that had once been the last window in the row, the one with the blinds up. It was gone, as was most of the window next to it, and the cold night air had filled the studio.

The creature had let him live and had, like some kind of burglar, disappeared into the night.

But it might come back.

That thought quickly cleared up the grogginess in his head and he left the studio, hurried down the hall, went into his bedroom, and flipped on the light. He pulled a large suitcase from the closet, flopped it onto the bed, and opened it. He quickly rummaged through his drawers and closet, stuffing clothes into the suitcase.

When it was full, he forced the suitcase closed, took all the money from his wall safe, grabbed his coat in the kitchen on the way out, and left.

Outside, he walked. He had no idea where he was going, only that he was going *away*. If it came back, he would not be there.

What if it doesn't come back?

Not my problem.

He picked up his pace.

What if it stays out there? You know what it's doing.

Not my problem.

You know it's hurting people. Killing them. Shedding their blood. Bathing in it.

At the next corner, he stopped and watched for a cab, started waving at the first one he saw. He focused on three words, like a mantra.

Not my problem. Not my problem. Not my problem.

Roses and Raindrops

Richard Chizmar & Brian Keene

Another child was killed yesterday...

And probably right around the time that it happened, I was sitting alone on my screened-in back porch, eating dinner and watching the storm break. A bowl of cabbage soup and a cheese sandwich taken right there on the porch. Too tired to even make it to the dining room table. I'm getting to be an old fart, can barely leave the damn house anymore. This weather makes me feel even worse, but I stayed out just the same and watched until the clouds drifted away. There might not be too many left for me. Not too much of anything left for me, so I like to see all I can.

It wasn't a big one. Not as far as storms go. Us folks here in Aberdeen, Virginia have seen much worse. I'd barely finished my soup when I noticed the wind letting up. Sure enough, a half-hour later, the rain slowed to a drizzle and the scattered line of baby evergreens along the north fence straightened and relaxed, while tiny waterfalls cascaded down onto their lower branches.

There hadn't been much thunder or lightning this time around either. Nothing special or impressive about this storm. Just a steady, depressing downpour; the kind that creeps through the walls of your house and seeps right into your bones; the kind that makes you want to crawl into bed and pull up the covers even though it's barely five in the afternoon.

So, no, it wasn't a big storm, especially not for Aberdeen. Lasted barely a handful of hours, and then went on its merry way up north toward our Yankee neighbors in Maryland. A lot of folks probably thought—*hoped*—that we had gotten lucky this time. Escaped without harm. But a lot of folks are damned fools.

We didn't get lucky. It happened again.

* * *

Another child was killed yesterday...

This is how it happened *this* time. At least, this is what Pecker Robbins overheard down at the Texaco station. Now, I know what they'll say about ol' Pecker. That he listens to Alex Jones and believes George Bush and Barack Obama are teaming up to send in United Nations soldiers to take away his hunting rifle. Far as I know, Bush spends his days on a ranch somewhere in Texas. And Obama? Well, I don't much care for him either, but the man has been in office eight years now and not yet has anybody shown up at Pecker's door and demanded his guns. So, I reckon he's wrong on that.

But not on this.

The call came in to police dispatch as the storm was winding down. Megan Bradley's husband, Jerry, told police that they had locked their daughter, Kassie, in her upstairs bedroom, soon as the storm first arrived.

Just to be safe, you understand.

Megan had unlocked the bedroom door shortly after six o'clock to serve Kassie her dinner and discovered that the girl was missing. The frantic mother checked the bathroom, underneath the bed, and inside the walk-in closet before noticing the curtains fluttering in the breeze. The bedroom window was open.

According to Pecker (who heard it from one of the responding officers), Megan called out for her husband—quietly at first, then shrieking with panic. At the sound of her voice, Jerry bounded up the stairs and stopped in the doorway, following his wife's wide-eyed gaze to the billowing curtains. Without a word, the couple— maybe gaining strength from each other's presence—moved forward together. Moved slowly, I reckon.

I imagine their footsteps made whispering sounds on the plush carpet. Knowing that a story is only as good as the details, Pecker recounted to me how the officer had described Kassie's bedroom. If I close my eyes, I can picture those poor parents inching past the pink-canopied bed, the neat desk with the laptop computer, her bookshelves lined with soccer trophies and those Harry Potter books.

They stopped in front of the open window. I'll bet the rain was louder there. Jerry reached out and pushed aside the soaked curtains—

—and there on the drenched windowsill, they found a single

red rose petal.

According to Pecker, that was when Megan fainted.

About an hour later, after the storm had ended, one of the responding officers found Kassie's remains in the Bradley's south meadow. Her tiny torso slit wide open from her neck right down to below her belly button. To no one's surprise, her eyes and ears were missing, as were her fingers and toes.

And, of course, just like all the times that had come before, they found—clinched between her crooked, little teeth—a single blood-red rose.

* * *

Another child was killed yesterday...

I know this whole business must sound strange to an outsider, but us folks here in Aberdeen have grown used to the storms and their deadly consequences. Over the years, we learned to fear the storms, loathe the storms with all our hearts. But we've also learned to accept them as part of our town's undeniable heritage.

Believe it or not, it doesn't get talked about much anymore. Times are tough the world over, and people around here know that. They also know that Aberdeen has somehow remained untouched by much of the problems that plague today's society. We don't have drugs or poverty. Our schools are good. The churches are full on Sunday. Property taxes stay pretty low. There are no terrorists training out in our cornfields. Hell, other than when the storms come, there's no crime to speak of. Maybe some teenagers driving too fast, or somebody getting drunk and starting a fight. Maybe some mischief come Halloween night. But that's small stuff. Folks here recognize that Aberdeen has somehow remained a prosperous place to run a business, to raise a family and put a roof over your head and three squares on the table every day. For a lot of folks, that's all that matters.

If you've got those things, you might tend to look the other way so that you can hold onto them. You might make excuses, become forgetful. You might even pretend.

For years, I wasn't one of those people. I often wondered to myself—worried to myself—about the small town I'd been born and raised in. Why had we been cursed to live in such fear? Why had none of us went and asked for outside help to solve this terrible mystery?

Although I never had any children to worry about—my Jenny couldn't have kids and it never mattered a lick to me, no sir—the questions troubled me on many a long and restless night.

Until nine years ago, almost to this very day, when—completely by accident—I discovered the answer.

It was the hottest summer I can remember—and believe me, I've seen a lot of summers—but by no means the driest. The storms hit us hard that year, and a half-dozen children were dead by mid-August.

I was still working at the mill then, putting in my ten hours a day and collecting a legitimate paycheck. I miss those days. You spend your life looking forward to retirement, and then, when it comes, you spend the rest of your days wishing you could go back. Life is tricky that way.

I remember it was a Thursday, just before quitting time, and Teddy Jenkins, the mill foreman, came into the shop and asked me to make a special delivery for him. He was all secretive about it. Whispered so the other workers wouldn't hear him. He said it was important and he would have done it himself, but he had an anniversary dinner planned with his wife and there was no way in hell he could miss it (if you'd ever set eyes on Teddy's wife, Mabel, you know he was telling the truth). Anyway, Teddy finished with a hearty pat on my back and said I was the only man he could trust to do the job right.

The whole thing struck me as a little strange—Teddy wasn't exactly the complimenting kind, and if there's one thing folks in Aberdeen can all agree on, it's that he didn't trust *anyone*—but I needed the overtime, so I obliged. Also, looking back, I reckon he played to my ego a bit.

I helped Teddy load my pick-up with a dozen sacks of mulch, another two dozen sacks of planting soil, and a stack of heavy two-by-fours. The bed sank a good few inches, and I wondered if my shocks would hold, but they did. Then he lowered his voice again—even though there was no one else around—and gave me directions to the house I was to deliver to. When he was finished, he made me repeat them to him. Twice.

I had never seen Teddy act like this before. Usually, he was loud and obnoxious. As I climbed into my truck, I looked at his expression and realized something.

He was scared.

It was in his voice and his eyes and the way he moved. Teddy Jenkins was terrified of something.

"Listen here," he growled, coming up to my driver's side window. "Drop the goods right there in front of the porch and be on your way without delay. These people pay good money and always on time. In return, I deliver their purchases and respect their privacy. You do the same. Understand?"

Puzzled and unsettled, I nodded my agreement and was on my way.

The evening was hot and sticky. The roads I was driving were rutted dirt, and bounced me around like I was riding on a rollercoaster at the State Fair. I waved to a little boy carrying a fishing pole on my way out of town, but the little bastard didn't even wave back. I just shook my head at him and kept on going. The truck radio was broken, so I had a lot of time to think during the drive, and my thoughts were dominated by Teddy's bizarre behavior. I decided there had to be a simple explanation to the whole thing. Just had to be patient and wait and see for myself.

I was heading west and deeper into the thick woodlands of the valley. I'd hunted the valley more times than I could count but always further south where the interstate ran. Same with fishing; the Hanson River held some of the finest smallmouth bass in the state, but all the best spots were located to the south. Dead west was a whole lot of dark forest and scrub brush. Despite having lived here all my life, it was new territory for me.

After ninety minutes of jostling around on those old dirt roads, I finally spotted the bent-over weeping willow with the red cross painted on its trunk just like Teddy had described. I turned left into a weed-choked driveway that wound its way through a tunnel of trees. The overhanging branches blocked out the sky, casting enough shadow that I had to turn on the headlights. The trees seemed to crowd the road, and I rolled up my window to keep the branches from slapping my arm.

I followed that dark, leafy tunnel for what had to be nearly a mile and had just about convinced myself that it was never going to end when it abruptly did just that—and I found myself in the sun again, squinting at a modest, nicely-kept log cabin perched in the middle of a gently-sloping, grassy hollow. I looked around but didn't see anyone outside. There were no cars out front. I parked by the porch, as Teddy had directed, and then got out.

"Hello?" I called, stretching.

There was no reply. I noticed then how quiet it was. Not even the whir of crickets or the chirps of birds in the surrounding woods. Only thing I heard was the ticking of my cooling engine.

Feeling unsettled, I lowered the truck bed and started unloading the planks of wood and sacks of mulch and soil. I glanced at the house as I worked, searching for a face in a window or any sign of movement. Nothing. I found myself working faster. I wondered who the hell these people were, and why they lived way out here in the middle of nowhere, without even a Wal Mart nearby. I mean, there's living in the country. Aberdeen is surrounded by farms and hunting cabins. But this? This was something else.

When I'd finished unloading, I decided to wait until I got home to sweep out the bed of my truck; no small decision for a man of my stubborn nature and work habits. But that unsettled feeling in my stomach had grown into a full-fledged case of the willies by then, and I just wanted to get the hell out of there.

I hopped in the driver's seat and put the key in the ignition—and then it hit me.

I had to pee.

If there's any single urge stronger than curiosity—or even fear—in a man of my age, it's the urge to piss. Like my Daddy used to say: *when you gotta, you gotta.*

I glanced back at the dark mouth of the tree tunnel, and decided I better get it over with right then and there. I've always said it was politer to piss in a man's backyard then his front, so I started around back. By that point, I'd pretty much convinced myself there was nobody home.

I rounded the corner. Cords of firewood were stacked eight-feet-high along the side of the house. Unusual, considering it was still summertime. I kept walking.

The back yard—it was more meadow than yard; a good three acres of trees had recently been cleared and stumps pulled up—was impressive. I stared in wonder, thinking: *it would have taken a work crew a full week and a ton of equipment to do that much clearing. How did they get the equipment back here?*

I had just about reached the tree line and was going for my zipper when I heard a sound behind me. Faint laughter. Coming from the house.

I forgot all about my need to pee. Forgot about Teddy's warning to respect their privacy, as well. I wanted to know what the hell was going on here. I quickly worked my way toward the back of the house. Without thinking, I edged closer and crouched down below a window. I heard more giggles. Clearer now. It sounded like a woman. Unable to resist, I inched up and peered over the windowsill.

And pissed my pants.

Piled on several plates in the middle of a big table were mounds of glistening body parts—blood-splattered ears, fingers, toes. And internal organs, too—long, slippery ropes of intestines and plump, shiny brown bags that were either livers or kidneys. I've field dressed enough deer in my time to know what organs look like. But these didn't belong to no deer. The stench was revolting, even muted through the wall. It reeked of foulness and sweetness at the same time—an electric tang not unlike the way a thunderstorm smells when it comes rolling in across the hills.

A wrinkled old couple danced around the cramped dining room, cackling with apparent glee, pausing only to gorge themselves with more mouthfuls of dripping morsels.

The old man said something I couldn't quite hear, and the woman laughed again, mouth open wide, revealing perfectly straight rows of white—albeit gore-stained—teeth. They had to be dentures. A woman that age? But no, they were her real teeth. If they weren't, then she had access to the greatest cosmetic dentist of all time. But it wasn't just her teeth that threw me. Her eyes, two brilliant blue sparks, twinkled like those of a young woman.

The old man skipped like a little boy into the next room and returned with a stained brown package. He unraveled it across the table revealing four human hearts.

The woman's eyes widened. She snatched one of the organs and bit into it like an apple, twisting her head back and forth like it was a particularly tough piece of beef jerky. Blood dripped from her fingers and chin.

The old man tilted his head and smiled lovingly as he watched her chew. It was that gesture that finally broke me. Of all the repulsive sights in that charnel house, it was that smile—and the adoration behind it—that scared me the most.

I turned and ran. I'm not ashamed to admit it. I made it about twenty yards before falling to the ground and puking. Stones and briars jabbed at my knees and palms, but I barely noticed.

I pushed myself up and started running again, and that's when I saw another patch of trees had been cleared on the opposite side of the house—and row after row of stunning, bright red roses grew in the carefully manicured dark earth. I stumbled to a halt and stood there shaking. The piss on my pants leg began to turn cold.

The old man inside that house had cleared the trees and stacked the firewood by himself; maybe the old woman had even helped. It wasn't Teddy Jenkins. It wasn't anyone from town. There was never a work crew up there. The old man and woman had cleared the trees themselves. They were old and wrinkled on the outside but eternally young and strong on the inside, where it counted.

They weren't human. They couldn't be.

They were monsters.

Immortal monsters draining the lives from our helpless children to somehow replenish their own.

Standing there at the edge of that garden, staring out over the dozens of flowers destined for innocent victims, frozen with fear and revulsion, it was too much. I got dizzy and my ears began to ring. Willing myself not to faint, I ran like hell, jumped into my truck, and barreled through that dark tunnel of trees without slowing.

Indeed, I didn't until I was out of that valley and back across the Aberdeen town limits.

And I've never been back there since.

* * *

Another child was killed yesterday...

I've never spoken a word about that day to anyone. I had a gut feeling—and gut feelings are usually right—that Teddy knew exactly what the hell was going on at that house. All of it. That would certainly explain his behavior that day. I never got the chance to ask him because he dropped dead not long after. Heart attack, down at the VFW. Fell right off his barstool and cracked his head open.

Nowadays, when I think about it, it almost feels like a dream. It feels like it happened a long time ago, when I was a younger man, but in the grand scheme of my life, it wasn't. And yet, that dreamlike feeling remains. As does my confusion. They say wisdom comes with age, but I've yet to gain an understanding of what I saw that day.

I don't know how long they've been up there, the old man and woman. Maybe forever. Maybe they were here before us. I don't know how it all started or when or even why. And I don't understand a damn thing about those awful roses. Maybe the old woman feels remorse for the killings and leaves the roses as tribute or remembrance; or maybe they enjoy the killings and the rose is simply a macabre calling card.

And there's one more thing that really puzzles me on those lonely, sleepless nights when I find myself wondering about this town I call my home and these people I call my neighbors.

I wonder about the storms.

I don't know, and that makes me angry and frustrated. I just can't make sense of them.

But then again, I can't do much of anything these days. Even need help getting to the shithouse when my arthritis gets cranky. Growing old? I don't recommend it. Friends and loved ones go off and die, leaving you lonely. Everything hurts, physically and emotionally.

Sometimes, when I sit on the back porch and watch the storms roll through and wait to hear if it's happened again, I can't help but remember how gracefully the old man moved across the floor; the gleam in the old woman's blue eyes, and how they stared at each other with such youthful love. It would be nice to feel that again. To feel anything, other than the aches in my joints and the loneliness in my heart. To dance again. To laugh. To have energy again.

To have an appetite.

And more and more every day, while I sit here alone waiting to die, rubbing my aching hands together, watching the children pass without so much as a wave hello anymore, I am tempted to somehow get back to that house again—and ask that old couple to let me join them.

Writer Biographies

Richard Chizmar

Richard Chizmar is the founder/publisher of *Cemetery Dance* magazine and the Cemetery Dance Publications book imprint. He has edited more than 30 anthologies and his fiction has appeared in dozens of publications, including *Ellery Queen's Mystery Magazine* and *The Year's 25 Finest Crime and Mystery Stories*. He has won two World Fantasy awards, four International Horror Guild awards, and the HWA's Board of Trustee's award.

Chizmar (in collaboration with Johnathon Schaech) has also written screenplays and teleplays for United Artists, Sony Screen Gems, Lions Gate, Showtime, NBC, and many other companies. He is the creator/writer of *Stephen King Revisited*, and his third short story collection, *A Long December*, is due in 2016 from Subterranean Press.

Chizmar's work has been translated into many languages throughout the world, and he has appeared at numerous conferences as a writing instructor, guest speaker, panelist, and guest of honor.

You can follow Richard Chizmar on both Facebook and Twitter.

Ray Garton

Ray Garton is the author of the classic vampire bestseller *Live Girls*, as well as *Scissors*, *Sex and Violence in Hollywood*, *Ravenous*, his new Moffet & Keoph investigation *Vortex*, and dozens of other novels, tie-ins, and story collections. He has been writing in the horror and suspense genres for more than 30 years and was the recipient of the Grand Master of Horror Award in 2006. He lives in northern California with his wife Dawn where he is at work on a new novel. You can find him online at raygartononline.com

Brian Keene

Brian Keene is the author of more than forty books, including *Darkness on the Edge of Town*, *Dead Sea*, *Dark Hollow*, *Ghoul*, and *The Rising*. Keene has also written for media properties such as *Doctor Who*, *The X-Files*, *Hellboy*, and *Masters of the Universe*. His numerous awards and honors include the World Horror Grand Master Award. He lives in Pennsylvania. You can find Keene online at briankeene.com

LampLight Volume 3

lamplightmagazine.com/volume-3

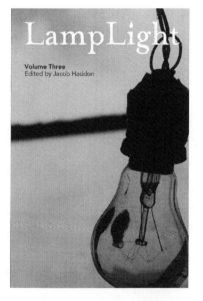

The third Volume of LampLight magazine, with issues from September 2014 - June 2015

Featuring the full novella by Kelli Owen, *Wilted Lilies*. Fiction and interviews with Yvonne Navarro, Mercedes M. Yardley, Nate Southard, Victorya Chase.

Fiction from:

Gary A. Braunbeck, Sana Rafi, Nick Mamatas, Roh Morgon, Tom Brennan, Salena Casha, Rati Mehrotra, J. J. Green, Damien Angelica Walters, Gwendolyn Kiste, John Boden, Kristi DeMeester, T. Fox Dunham, Davian Aw, John Bowker, Kealan Patrick Burke

Subscriptions, Past Issues and Submission information at
LampLightMagazine.com

A Night at Old Webb

apokrupha.com/OldWebb

By Kevin Lucia

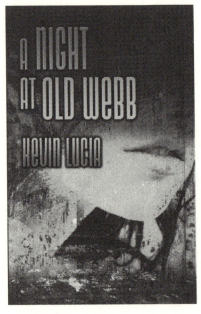

Old Webb, an abandoned grammar school just outside Clifton Heights, is the place to be late summer nights in Webb County. A gathering place for friends to be themselves, away from grownups who have forgotten what it means to be young and free.

The summer of 1992, Kevin Ellison spent his Saturday nights there like everyone else. Everything was running according to plan: a college basketball scholarship, school, all the things everyone expected of him.

Then he met a girl named Michelle Titchner, and everything changed...

Made in the USA
Middletown, DE
19 February 2024

50049305R00035